Jennie Allida Dickenson

Pluto In Capricorn

The Poems

Pluto's transit through Capricorn started in 2008 as I was trying to find my way as an adult. 20 years old. Pluto brings transformational energy, in my case near my seventh and eighth house cusp. This energy impacted relationships, intimacy and emotional dependencies from 2008-2024 in its fifteen year cycle. The eighth house is about depth, transformation and merging with others. Pluto had me deeply examining my partnerships, or lack thereof; a journey of deep vulnerability. Pluto is also about uncovering hidden truths, I have discovered and discarded so much in the last fifteen years! Faced fears, abandonment, betrayal, power struggles, grappled with trust and this collection of poems that spans these past fifteen years reflects the journey.

The areas of my natal chart affected by Pluto also included my relationship with finances, if you know me it hasn't been an easy financial journey in the last fifteen years. I have gone through quite a few jobs trying to find my niche while always desiring to simply be a silversmith. I always wondered if I would have had an easier time at everything if I could have gotten a handle on my finances, but I have to remind myself I have been working hard for my hourly wages this entire time. I am hoping for a shift in this space soon as I follow what I feel are my true gifts…I was pretty good at every job I held, but I don't believe I was destined to be a chef, snake wrangler, construction worker or correctional officer.

I have been asked to consider the thought experiment of going back in time, I would say not even one minute. I am always looking forward to the future and it almost seems silly to expose these poems, like I should just burn them and move on. I wanted to publish them anyway to mark the end of this cycle and the beginning of a beautiful new one. I am no longer worried about what anyone knowing my struggles and inner thoughts would think about it. Pluto has transformed all my Capricorn placements and I am assured of my self integrity and autonomy. I have a deeper understanding of myself and my connection to others, and lovers. I am fully my authentic resilient self through the intensity and tribulations of the last fifteen years.

This collection spans the gamut of all emotions, many themes are explored and I hope you enjoy reading them. In the future I will be writing happy love poems, a romantic true story novel and other such drivel as I have found someone who is very brave to be in love with. I can't wait to live, write and share the new paradigm I am stepping into.

PS the poems featured here have been scrambled in order of years and such to try to protect the identity of the innocent as much as possible.

With Gratitude!!!
Jennie Allida Dickenson

Radical Appreciation

You make me feel
Like the
End all
Be all
And the
Beginning.

Jennie Allida Dickenson

Flipside

My brother looked at me
Clear logical
Understanding
That understands me.
Like no assurety I have ever known.
Knowing and said
I don't know.
And I stood up
Under those interrogative eyes
OK yes
I do know in fact.
Laid down my prediction.

I feel a deep peace
In knowing we will all see each other on
The flipside.
And I'll flip tables
If y'all disagree
And talk you down to see
Your reflection
Will get you to where you need to be
Seeing yourself as divinity.

Jennie Allida Dickenson

WHEN I THOUGHT I COULD HEAL THE MATTER I MAGICALLY LOST THE ABILITY TO FIX THINGS

2011

I was notorious
Paranoid
Sure the PD had it out for me.
No scheduled vacation
Riding my bike like a demon
Tires kicking up clouds of trailing reputation
People knew where to find me.
Recently healed scars, bruises
Wondering how many I counted as friends
Bar tabs bigger than my paycheck
Couldn't sweep the dirt out of the cracks.
The spectre of respect haunted me with its reflection
Windexed, my faults streaky.
A to do list I longed to be crossed off.
My effort like the lawn was patchy.
Low energy, fueled on covertly rolled spliffs and coffee.
My love scorned publicly with karaoke
"Next time baby, I'll be bulletproof.."
Rumors tendrilled others interest in me
Hoping it didn't stick around the ankles of my boots.
My finances fractions of what I needed
A third of what I desired
Spent wholly on my destruction.
I longed to spend my time on the roof,
Where I could observe without having to participate.
Fruit hung heavy on the tree
I thought about shooting myself in the basement everyday.
Figuring there would be an entrance fee free gate to hell there.

Jennie Allida Dickenson

Jameson made my forced joviality real
For the hours before I rode to the desert
Out amongst the sage every night
I sat and reeled in a wild uncontrolled state
Wishing to keep riding
Pedal away out of sight.
So hateful of myself I tried to give myself away
But no one would take
What they couldn't trust.
A new event on the calendar was an admonishment waiting to happen.
I tried to drown out the creaking sighs of the building,
Groans calling for help
by singing.
When told to be quiet
You could hear my every step with bottles clinking
My path marked with a twinkling cacophony
Of drunken oblivion to look forward to.

Jennie Allida Dickenson

Inherent Danger

I am frankly tired of pining away.
And I want to get down to the business
Of loving you.
I have little time
And a million years
I am a well of patience
Also a roaring all consuming wildfire.

Part of our courting
Is exposing my neck
The risk
The inherent danger
A ritual
To show dedication
And lack of fear
Demonstrating freedom.

Yes
I do
Choose
You.

Jennie Allida Dickenson

5D SLEEP

When you are in my bed
And I am cuddled against you
I can't ask for a safer
More comfortable feeling.

I dream vividly that you turn to me
Wrap your strong arms around me.
That you allow me to deeply kiss you
Sighing my pleasure into your mouth
While your appetite rises to meet me.
My whole body burns with passion next to you.
My body jumps in anticipation of its own accord
And I can feel you are here deep inside of me.

When I wake
You aren't far
Your back turned
And I shake off the
Dance
With your higher self.

Jennie Allida Dickenson

Imagination

The imagination is a powerful thing,
I seem to recall perfectly a kiss
You say didn't happen.

I could have imagined how exactly you taste,
The shape and texture of your lips.
In my mind I experienced it.
I imagine you've imagined too.

Mirror images
Moving in sync
A dance you can't hide your knowledge of
It's as natural to you as the heave of a heavy sigh
Breath through lungs
Water to the parched and dry

Here we are ignoring the perfection of nature.
Staying uncomfortably rolled to one side
A turtle on its back.

When I kiss your fingers
I want you to open your fist
Go completely slack
To my adoration
And soak it in.

Showering caresses, explorative kisses,
You are still wearing your jacket and boots.

My imagination rides me
The way I know you want to.

Jennie Allida Dickenson

Every delectable thought heats my coursing blood.
All your inner reasoning cannot temper me
Or slow my desire.
Yes, I am imagining, psychic
You, however, can tell me no.
And with respect, I'll withdraw into my own mind.
BUT I can't help but overhear!

When I am sure I can stand, I try.
My legs go slack shaking
You stand admiring
Smiling
Knowing
Exactly what I was thinking.

The air has a crisp violence in it
The smell of fall
I smile a bit back
Knowing that every step forward I take
No matter what
Will seem like an attack.
I am aching for the day you try to get me back.

You have a well hidden sadistic streak.
I do want you to pin me down and make me squirm.
All the other women in the world
But trying to figure you out makes me tick.

We both feel balanced on the edge
To cut asunder
Or to fall in?

Love,
Can you imagine?

Jennie Allida Dickenson

Aphrodite

It is a powerful man that has a woman unashamed
To appear in front of her parents
Smelling and looking like Aphrodite
Ravished within an inch of immortality.

Truly I died one death
That of any thought of another man.

Appearing out of the ocean
Brined, ready and open
Awaiting my warrior
With a parted lip grin
Of pure
And honest
Desire.

Jennie Allida Dickenson

Harsh Realities

I had a dream about you
Where I opened your bedroom door.
While I was knocking
Simultaneously apologizing.
Feeling intrusive
You never responded.
I came and sat
At your left hand side.
You pulled out a needle
Full of dark liquid
I asked gently,
as you started injecting,
What was contained,
"Harsh realities".

I started to write
My right hand
Moving towards you
As you settled into the effects.
As my hand got closer
You took it in yours
Brought it to your lips
and kissed it.

Jennie Allida Dickenson

MATRIARCH

They'd call you crazy
A fool to chance me
To find the silver lining
In this madness
To find peace in the chaos
Of the organized mess I keep.

I have to be a good example for my sisters.
Show them what true love is and looks like.
I want to tell them that it exists.

I just felt my mother's pain
So real so raw
Rare power
And grace in form.

Inheritance of all of our grandmother's.

She is everything I aspire to.
And I don't desire the credit either,
I want to be the unseen glue
A hidden rivet
The solid connection
A cupping bezel
The family jewel
MATRIARCH

Jennie Allida Dickenson

BRIDE

The sweet yoke
The light burden
Of divine law.

I take you into my heart of hearts
With beneficent fortitude.

Do I cross your mind?
Actively feeding your dreams?
As devoted, beautiful, wise
Your happiness and success.
As a good mother?

The best I can hope to achieve
Is to become the spiritual bride of a just man.
You read the law,
I interpret it.
The bright reflection of the divine mother.

Behind you is any competition for my affections
At the foundation you have already won them.
To stand at the last judgement
Side by side with me
Judged worthy of
Eternal life.

But for now you shy away from me.
Delay or absence?
I know you.
Dedicated to the highest good,
Possessing of the gifts of a poet.

Jennie Allida Dickenson

You are living the idea of gain
To build a house and family.
Hoping to craft it skillfully, perfectly.
Fearing that you might be mistaken in me.

I have assurety
You have discernment
Your heart is safe with mine
And your success a certitude.

Don't let your attempt
To penetrate the Mystery of God overwhelm you.

Jennie Allida Dickenson

SONG 2

September 28, 2019

L'alm al-mein, amen.

Love absolutely cannot be lost
Forgiving is its only cost
Though your heart feels
Rent and tossed
Master of myself
I am boss.
To partners I only frost.
My tough exterior is gloss.
I swore I saw you
Through the sheen
An aura had me believe you were him.
Visiting me in all of my pleasant dreams.
Was it you or me
Meant to redeem?
Crazy I know
In conversation it seemed
You gave me every reason to sing.
I was sure you could protect me,
Sure I am so fine,
Damn all this attempted poaching.
I am lost and we found me.
Gloss a veil shining delightedly.

Jennie Allida Dickenson

Song ONE

Outside Of Los Angeles CA
Written on the back of a hitchhiking sign
May 30th 2011

Maybe I just developed a thicker skin
Couldn't decide whether soul, real or thoughts I am in.
Swimming upstream to some ancient home,
People yelling what's wrong with your dome?
That's the long way, that's the wrong way,
And you girl will never find your way home.
Y'all laugh and joke when I say I have futuristic dreams.
Read your tarot? Hardly.
I've heard harpie, witch, snitch, bitch, pitcher so which is which?
I sing and live in dreams, It is all it seems!
You should try it, open your heart and mind
Let them wander, set them free!
You'll forget those names, every name you had.
I want you to see so you will also be glad.
And though the purple gray dusk will settle
Worry will sweep your brow,
Just grit your teeth and remember mettle.
Just like unsinkable Molly Brown,
This is Jennie Dee, never going down.

Jennie Allida Dickenson

MEDITATIONS ON LOVE AND FEAR

December 21st, 2015

You are afraid.
Is it a matter of self love
Or lack thereof?
I am Brave
Crashing waves
On your bulkhead
We are afraid
We both get it.
How terrifying and wonderful it could be
Shadowy dealings
Exalted to great heights
We toy with courage
Flashing one card
From our hand
at a time.
I want to breathe fire into you.
However it is a war crime
When you are curled
As a snake in a hole.
So you desire to command?
Mete out judgement?
Be king?
Your sword holds no sway.
To be king you need no queen.
You need justice.
Real weight behind your words
A moral high ground
And impeccable ethics. I
Rare as a fairy gift.
To be our fearless leader

Jennie Allida Dickenson

Take my light
Bathe in it
Tend roses
of blooming self awareness
Grow gardens of spirituality
Flames joined getting higher
In concord, sharing harvest
Friendship evolving into union.
Sharing sympathy on each other's porches
A natural passion
Our nature exalted
And in the glow of moonlight
Sanctified.
I will continue to rule
My kingdom as Empress
Embodying the every desire of man
Until you realize
That as daughter of
Heaven and Earth
I can be your freedom
And your victory.
There is no time for fear
Embody love
Rise in response
Answering
transformational summons.

Jennie Allida Dickenson

SACRAL

It is disturbing to me
That a thought of you
Casually spurred.

Awakens my root chakra with a
THUMP

This desire unknown to me
Someone I don't know
Stoking a fire from afar
Just by existing

Who lit it?

When we happen to meet
The steady thumping
Turns kundalini rising
You have the eyes of Horus

If I shine when I am with you
And your aura awakens near me
And I thump along steadily
Fed by the idea of you
Why haven't we merged?

Jennie Allida Dickenson

Fear on your part and minet ready to share myself
Fearful of losing the
 Solitude
I fought for
Distrust of such obvious portends.
You can't approach
The object of your desire
With an attitude of fear.

So I am facing them all down.
Made brave by the beat of my
Internal war drum.

The deep bass of my root chakra
Sending out call and reply.

Thrumming along, fires stoked.
Our hearts know the tune
Our bodies instrumental
Our song is life.

Jennie Allida Dickenson

5-6-18

Thinking about it so much
That I can see you with my open eyes
The veil
A vision hovering before me
Your face in angelic bliss
Ecstatic smiles
The brush of a beard
I haven't felt yet
On my cheek an energetic imprint.

Holding the vibration in my core
Shaking me without release.
Thoughts of you in palpable energy
Holding me still
Till they spur us
Into action.

Jennie Allida Dickenson

Aquarian Season

In the Aquarian season
When the water bearer darkens skies.
And the bright sun is a brief welcome respite.
A waning gibbous moon
brings the hope of new intentions to be made.

The peach trees bloom
And all the glory is budding out.
A Light bearing moon
Seen in the morning
Is fresh momentum.

Dark moon Lilith
Exposes karmic patterns to be released
And the sun bleaches the bones
Death is as much a feminine archetype
As birth and creation are.

Saturnalia prodding your everyday
self sabotage based on perceived chains.
Find power in knowing freedom
Is not given
 it is taken.

The constant
yet ever changing
 Phases of the moon
Reflect for us the wisdom
Of deliberate progress
Erosion.
the sense of urgency
Is a hindrance.

Jennie Allida Dickenson

Fear
A sinking feeling of
Panic deep into your body
Your root chakra should be warm coals to be stoked
Not heavy cold stone
Cryptic pluto
In cahoots with Saturn
Will force you to stand
Transmute your terror
Or be thrashed.

Square off
Be brave
remember there is no
"impossible" !!
gifts of luck
come from jupiter.
Enjoy the waxing gibbous moon unfolding.

As earth is shaken
Rent and torn
Outer planets aligning
Conjuncting
Welcome your confusion.
Peace is knowing everyone is your teacher
Whether you like the lesson or not.

Silent and alone
I gaze on the craters of Cynodia
Contemplating my origin
In the stars
At once everything
And singular
Love from an eternal well.

Jennie Allida Dickenson

Mars' rusty hue
Adorns the Eastern sky in the predawn hours.
Your fate is your own
meddling in conflict
Will complicate your journey.

In a week
I will use the lit side of the crescent moon
To find mercury
Dimly shining at the horizon point at sunset
It is Confidence in communication
With stars as messengers
fortitude is key

Find the planet of love
Venus
In the Western sky at sunset.
Dancing with Neptune
The higher octave of love
Divinty
 my exalted ruling planet.
Promise me you will continue
To dream up possibilty

The moon and yourself
In luminescent flux.

Jennie Allida Dickenson

BEETLES

I dreamt you gave me a rusting platter
Of those mysterious red beetles
That are killing the mountain ash in our backyard.
I hear all this music and can't find a source.
Tell myself I must be crazy,
And I will hide it well.
Hiding from myself behind headphones
Hangovers and long walks.
In love with unconscious dreams
Where I run an old western boardinghouse
Overseeing transient acquaintances.
Drinking whiskey.
Days where I wake smoking soberness
Surrounded by broken chains
Metal slices what your dreams were first made of,
Mettle seems to be all that I lack.
Weighing my changes on a scale
Against the platter of beetles
You ceremoniously presented me.
Beetles of doubt
Eating from the inside out
Dreams that will uproot me.

Jennie Allida Dickenson

SCHEMES

I allowed myself to dream
Of riding my bike in North Beach.
Drinking africanos in Cafe Trieste.
I was transported back to my schemes
Of being the cool intellectual chick who made your bling
And realized my hands had lost the callous of writing.
Gained the rough edge of hard work.
A new unthinking, just living, cooking, singing.
My fast and loose jive trying to control the nightmares
Of a ticking 'bout to blow!
Timed bomb
Of forgotten dreams,
Recurrent nightmares
And an archaeology dig.
What could be me?
What could be us?

Jennie Allida Dickenson

PAGE OF WANDS

Honorable
Afraid you won't be successful
Weighted with doubt
Sinking without trying to swim.

You are cross examining me
Vigilant in protection of your feelings.
Perhaps you have found me worthy
Or are willing to discover.

You are past seeking that which has vanished.
You've put your indecision behind you.
Looking forward.

You are all thought
Desperately clawing down your animal nature.
Intellectual, let peace into your thoughts.

You are operating from a place of violent chagrin.
And if there is scandal around me
Know I offer forgiveness.

Hope in expectation.
Apprehension in disloyalty
Fearful of opening your heart to the enemy.

Thus the indefinite delay.
You are responsible with your feelings and mine,
Useful yet discouraging.
Placidly studying my every message,
I'd love to know what you decide.

Jennie Allida Dickenson

CULPRIT

If we both the more,
Wanted the life of a poet
We could just fall in love.
Each other as muse
Would offer enough in this existence.
We could sing planets to beings
Orbit creativity
From ourselves as our own creations
Children or houseplants
Everyday would be a sonnet,
Love
Someone witty
As of me
Hep
To you
Resurrect the lost art form
Of writing
Gin and journeys
It is all a mystery.
Are you the partner in crime
To my culprit?

Jennie Allida Dickenson

DICHOTOMY OF SEPARATE

Becoming self aware is hard to do.
I just took a long good look at myself.
I am in love with myself
And that mirror that you are.
You have shown me

With doubt
With continual reassurance.
The dichotomy of our separate
Is my wholeness reflected
Back at me
The total freedom
And ultimate bondage
Of the self
And it's reflection.

Jennie Allida Dickenson

TOOL ROOM

There are thirteen hammers in the tool room
Monkey wrenches of all sizes.
A tool box completely full of rusted objects.
An axe, a drill press, over a dozen types of saws
A drawer of screwdrivers.
And I wish I could use the level to see if I am level headed
One of the eight measuring tapes
To measure the distance between here and happiness.
The excess of caulk on my foundation
To keep me from leaking,
Fix all these cracks.
Use the files to smooth over my tough facade.
Rewire my whole brain with the box of electric supplies.
Put up some of the extra gutters to catch the overspill of emotions
And funnel it somewhere safely.
But all I can do is put on the safety glasses, gloves and welding hat.

Jennie Allida Dickenson

PINNED

Significant desire
My will and determination
The significant problem is
That I want
You to be my significant other.
The lovers

If you see me as a willing and conscious temptress
I can't help it.
I know that I am providence
Offering to you
Through my imputed lapse
The way to arise ultimately.

I want you to try painting the pictures you have in mind.
Our mutual healing as the groundwork we've laid.
Becoming whole unto ourselves.
Virgins

Many endings in the past
Everytime circumstance
Rendered apart
Lifetimes unfulfilled
This is behind us.

From where I stand I can only see the fight.
Do I continue to try to convince you?
And myself
This is all that is
Wholly wonderful.

Jennie Allida Dickenson

Striving, wracking my brain
Trying everything
To be better, excellent.
Perhaps I am disingenuous
Vain and untrue.
Or perhaps I am skilled
Perfect as I am.

I exist in perfect conformity with nature
At its finest highest art.
And I believe you do too.
Aware of my nature
Aware of you
Faults, flaws, foibles
All recognized!

And besides
I want to join spirits
Consciously reunite our soul.
A grand hope that this would be ecstasy
Our perfect contentment
Fearing it to be merely comfortable.

If I have courage
I could gain your affections
Trust in our intimacy.
Haste
I won't wait another moment
For our assured felicity.

Let me be struck by the swift arrows of love
Pinned together
Rather than split
Anxious and indecisive.

Jennie Allida Dickenson

October Thirteenth

Sitting here watching the moon rise
I miss you
After a couple hours
A whirlwind of feeling right.
A grace for the needy
That didn't expect the gift.
Unexpected power in the feeling
That your moonlit face
Gracing my pillow
Sent reverberating to my core
Dreams fulfilled
And prayers answered
When asked right.
At dawn
At dusk
When the moon rises
Waxes or wanes
With gratitude at already expecting
The full manifestation.
But being thoroughly surprised
And delighted!
When he walks through the door.

Jennie Allida Dickenson

EXPLODED

I can't even quantify
The quantum leaps
Of love.
I am always astounded
That my love can get deeper
Wider
More expansive.

I have felt ready to burst at the seams
And it hasn't happened yet.
My heart will thud so resoundingly
I am sure it has exploded.

yet , here it is pounding
Away unforgivingly
So sweetly
And I haven't exploded, yet.

Just racing.

Jennie Allida Dickenson

DTF

I usually get to decide who I will heal,
But you healed me,
And I didn't even know I needed it.

So tough
So fucked up

And the first time I know it was pity
But the vortex of wild
Shot me back at you
A gust of down to fuck
That no one.
I mean no one
Would dare step in front of
Only those on grand death defying adventures.
I hadn't met someone quite like me in a long time.
Which was probably part of the healing
No death defying stunts but once a year
For a couple years
No ultimate heartbreak
For a damn while
Being terrified of such occurrences
I self sabotage in some way
But you took control
And gave me a real
Healing kundalini boost.
A powerful gift of ascendancy.
I started taking those first steps
Making my own way.
Not because of you
But you definitely gave me
an adjustment.

Jennie Allida Dickenson

OLD WEST

In the week I have been back in Elko
I have managed to exhaust myself with physical labor,
Get raucously drunk every night,
Been offered the esteemed position as Madame
of the number one Geisha,
And take Jesse James to bed.
Thinking about all this
While riding my pony Radish
I say to myself: Damn!
This is the old West.

Jennie Allida Dickenson

100% Acetate

If I ever spontaneously combust
I will be wearing Sarah Sweetwater's 100% acetate shirt.
A stray match flick
Explosion of hair
And whole body into oblivion
I always carry at least
Two lighters in my pocket.
Two small blasts sending bottle cap shrapnel
towards my cigarette smoking compadres,
Observing behind their own burning embers.
A quick thinking lad
throws his jameson on the rocks on my flames
Right as the jameson in my gullet ignites
Silver starts clinking to the ground
Till all that is still standing
Is my feet and calves in my magic boots
Which run off promptly
Away from the ash.

Jennie Allida Dickenson

DRIVEL

I feel divinely inspired one moment
Then it's back to drivel
Rather quickly.
I practice writing automatically so my thoughts don't get ahead of me and slip away.
Like a damn song slips away.

It's tough being in love.
That is
Unrequited.
Really distracting
Hoping is an almost futile task
That you have to do
It's homework
Chores
And essential
Like breathing
And sometimes brushing and flossing
Instinctual
Trying not to drown.

Realizing your karma
Only because it slaps you in the face
Really hard
You pour blood
I am trying to calculate my blood loss.

But it probably overflows
Tonight is the first freeze of the season.
I am going to stay here
And get used to it.
Really enjoy solitude.

Jennie Allida Dickenson

RASHIDA

Half mumbling
She pulled the hat way down.
And my mind filled in what I couldn't over hear
Wind whipped and laughing.
I learned in these spaces.
The rhythmic flow of our banter
Brought meaning to
The white moths that hexed my path
And swirling clouds
That inhabit my dreams.
An understanding forged in friendship
Encouraging me to tap my primal knowing
To speak without thinking
Telling me of your past life as a native
Recounting yourself as ancient
And I believe it when you tell me,
"I will see you
Next rotation."

Jennie Allida Dickenson

Poet and you didn't know it…

The text message that got me ghosted…

"Ya know. I felt a physicality about my life before knowing you.
Biblically
But now I feel a grander ... physicality about my life.
It's been a strange new thing.
I have all this threatening opposing male sexuality in my life.
Fearful, imposing.
And I knew that when I did dabble in that sort of physicality again I wanted it to be mutual,
possibility, divine, sensual, gratifying grandness.
And I am glad, as heck.
Been happy buzzing about all week.
But as I am prone to such daftness,
I am going to wait and wonder.
Vibrating alive,
attuned to an excitement about the weekend.
And seeing you."

Jennie Allida Dickenson

Samhain

I started my celebration like any true feast, three days beforehand. That's how long preparation takes. Gathered myself and my gear. On the auspicious date I meditated on my appreciation of Gaia, earth, our mother. Grateful for the growing season which is now ending. In which I grew immensely, the scope is yet to be delved. The tap root is deep, and the pot is shallow. Planted firmly in the ground, with a new moon, there is intention in everything I do. I am finally ready to unveil my intention. I am dry, falling seed in the best rain, ripe. Having dug the deepest holes, working at it, roots and vines have been overcome.

Might seem I am dormant. Sad, dead. Soon in some season there will be profuse bloom. I want you to appreciate the finality of the beauty right before the temperature drops and "changes" everything. A full harvest.

I want you to step back. See the beauty, away from the rush of the season. Realize the striking glory of the year you just lived and survived; a falling leaf or needle striking you firmly right in the mid brow. Awake. And see.

The death and potentiality that lies before ye.

I personally am in the darkest purging times. All of the chaff is sloughing. I am the gladdest I have ever been. Glad I survived ten days and looking forward to ten more. Slapping down my hand! Betting on the best without looking at it! Can you feel the positivity? It's for air, thought, dreams, doubts, the truth, lies, every bit that I can remember and memory itself. Samhain.

With the changing of the seasons we need to shore up our possibilities and potentialities. Hunker down for cold weather.

Reassess yourself, the environment and your survival. It's my favorite time when I have the time. I took the time today. Store away everything that I have spent countless hours preserving through the heat, the hot, the shit, the lava, the burning of the sun, all the water I carried, all the effort that I effort. Every bit of guilt and sagging dry leaf effort to save what I had a hand in keeping alive.

Do that for yourself. Now. Shelter, protect and nurture the creature and its extensions you have built through seasons. The dark cold winter is coming. And it can be a hibernation of thought, gently creative if you allow.

I am asking for a "full send" nostalgia for your own sake, because you will never ever ever be the same.

Nor will anything. Samhain.

Jennie Allida Dickenson

VOLUNTEER COMMISSARY PIRATES

You will be fastidious about washing your hands.
If you are sick, or don't feel well, do not push through!
Alert Jennie so proper precautions can be taken.
Hangovers don't count.
All wild hair needs to be secured, tied back, even hatted down perhaps.
Closed toe shoes! For dirty toes not to get possibly burnt or smashed.
We will be saving the food scraps for compost.
This is a tight budget for food so there will be no waste.
[No chopping veggies in a stupid way]
We will be prepping further meals while preparing current meals
so be tracking.
NO knives will be left in dish water!!!!
and will always be washed first and secured.
Have fun, and singing is encouraged.
Safety third.
Ask questions.
Aprons are functional and stylish

Jennie Allida Dickenson

West to East

Mysterious poet that wanders the sceptered isle

Turning away sharp words

By his prose and poetry

Like some latter day Lancelot

Honeyed voice reciting wisdom

From the ages

A man of the west traveling east

Spreading light for his fellow man.

Jennie Allida Dickenson

Love Effulgent

I am effulgent skipping through the woods this morning

thinking appreciative thoughts

of the powerful masculinity that picked me up and carried me to bed.

The cerulean eyes that don't shy away from looking into mine.

Passionate embrace, locked gaze

Ecstasy breathed into sound

"Oh, my god"

Speaking you as my providence.

Devotion penetrating my core

Our bodies as altars

Friction as worship betwixt

Gratitude welling up from my depths

As his strong arms steady

My shaking electric self

That can no longer stand on her own.

Bent over singing my supplication

Till I am brought to my knees

To swallow the sacrament of you.

Tasting divinity

Consecrating union.

Love effulgent.

Jennie Allida Dickenson

Duck and Dodge

I polished off the whisky.

I am sure you'll never talk to me again!

so I may as well tell you what I think:

I think you are scared of love.

I saw it in your eyes.

You may have heard something second hand

warned off me

I may be blocking the whole thing subconsciously

terror of losing an ounce of my freedom.

We could be embraced in ecstatic bliss

But we have insecurities to deal with!

I may fear that I may be delusional and seeking love somewhere it won't ever exist.

While you dodge a broken heart that an eighth and a handle couldn't fix.

Silly to duck and dodge what's ever meant for the two to coexist.

Right now all we are doing is hardening edges,

sharpening blades against a reality that doesn't have to exist.

We could simply come together in a kiss.

Jennie Allida Dickenson

Joseph's Opinion

I went to see Joseph, he told me all sorts of uncomfortable truths. Harsh

Some I accepted and some were more opinion. He told me that I am getting old and may be ripe but about to rot.

He told me I was not an ideal modern shape

My Venus de Milo body is too curvy and soft for the modern man.

That the aspects I refuse to change about myself are a sick form of torture that I carry in guilt because I think I am undeserving.

It was very constructive really. Despite how badly some of it made me feel. To face the shadow parts of yourself you must uncover them.

But we did have a disagreement. He said that women by nature are disloyal. And that true loyalty doesn't exist in womankind. I disagreed vehemently. And he pointed out that no one has given me the opportunity to prove him wrong. My mother said that's a belief held by men about women as an excuse to be disloyal themselves.

Joseph had great insight into why I push men away so quickly. It is my desire and excitement. I throw myself all in and give myself over everything as an offering and it's too much for most. It's not a chase for the man, he gets overwhelmed with the gift. Devalues it because he didn't have to earn it. It's also just hella creepy.

He said it's not really my fault as I am sort of inexperienced because I have never been successful in the havingness to know what a relationship is like. So I wouldn't understand how off putting my romantic nature is.

He told me I was naive and ridiculously innocent for being 32. He told me I have the morals I have because I want a moral high ground. And I disagreed with that too, because I truly believe that some things are just wrong or right.

The string of fate can be tangled and make yourself a noose if you don't know to be patient. Let it gently guide or cut it with Atropos scissors.

Jennie Allida Dickenson

Date Night

I tried to do my hair pretty.

Blonde it out a little,

Curl it up well

I bought red lipstick

The committed kind

After admiring myself for a moment

The dissonance of a done up face

Sent me to a panic

Had to use oil to get the 24 hour wear

Of it off my thin lips

They stained a rich darker color than normal

Which I ended up liking.

I'd bought new mascara

Bambi eyes, made my blonde lashes visible,

so much longer now they have grown out from the burn.

I bought new razors yesterday to prepare

I shaved carefully.

I had been niamiciding the hell out of my butt cheeks for a week

not to have any stray acne from my dirty 16 hour days

Hiking miles and miles in the woods

Sitting in the dirt

Napping in the pine needles

I used a turmeric mask on my whole body

I risked my enamels health

Jennie Allida Dickenson

Whitening tobacco and coffee stained teeth.

Managed to choose correctly

A shade of foundation that matched!

did a reasonable job of smoothing

The worried lines of my face.

Slathered myself in a rich lotion

To smooth my skin soft

To adhere the less than .5 ounce of perfume I own.

Plucked, shaved, or annihilated

My mustache, beard, nose

And stray eyebrow bits.

"Beauty is pain" ,

My dad used to tell me

when he brushed my hair as a child.

Feeling excellent

From the level of stretch and sweat

I achieved during my yoga session.

I chose a green dress

You have yet to see

And My ostrich boots

No control top needed

I wore some nice under things

But not as nice as the cursed set.

Hedging my bets.

Listening to a new album.

I strapped my belt to its tightest

Jennie Allida Dickenson

Self made hole,

Admired my waist.

Set off to get my nails done.

Spent a Jackson

On a dark purple queen vibe manicure

Anxiously waiting for my Fanny

pack to buzz with a reply

The utter disappointment

Of a cancelation.

I buy ten beers on my way home

Ipa 6.8%

And a light six pack to mitigate the damage on my midriff

that I worked all week to slim and tighten.

Relaxed into lonely

"And a dinner plan?!?"

Canceled in the next breath

Makeup, effort and hopes

Dashed with a wave

Salt water is the best exfoliant.

You'll look young and naive

Dumb and glorious.

Jennie Allida Dickenson

Nonchalant

It's been days without any reassurance of a message

Weeks without sight or feel of you

Usually the power of the spell of man wears off after two weeks

Some scientific fact I read up on whilst researching what to do

Now I really don't know what to do

I have never so deeply freaked myself out at the possibility of loss

Usually I cry for days and get over it

Then spend a month or two humbling my heart of it's bitterness

healing it back open and kind.

Becoming brave enough to try again.

This time feels different.

The literal physical sensation of my pain is wracking me.

my days of crying haven't dulled the edge.

I am sure you were my heaven sent felicity.

The failure to treasure

hold and understand

seems like a sin beyond measure.

I think of all the ways I must have hurt you

How I must have driven you away with my seeming nonchalance and brazen attitude.

Trying to seem cool and successful instead of revealing my vulnerability.

How much more honest could I have been?

I could have said everything I wanted to say.

I could have told you I loved you before it was too late.

Choking on the phrase every time because I thought it was too early.

Jennie Allida Dickenson

Heartbeat

My heart is beating out of my chest

Beating fast furious

At the idea of trying to explain myself

Of even sending you a message

I want to smooth over any roughness

I don't want to be at the drop of a hat tearful and fearful at having lost you

I lay down still

Let the cold air breath with me

Deep calming breaths

And my heart won't listen to my mind

It keeps its pounding

A literal bounce that shakes my frame.

I keep telling myself I have been deceived

By my own self

My mind keeps telling my heart to calm down

And it refuses to listen.

A powerful physical override of my conscious system.

Jennie Allida Dickenson

If He Wanted To, He Would

I don't think you understand!

The immense pain and suffering

That silence is

One note to say.

"Not today."

And I would cry a bit,

But be happy for a reply.

I want it to rain all day.

I want the sky to be like

My naive trusting dumb blue eyes

After they looked at you too long.

Precipitation and thunderous sobs

Reverberations felt in my chest

I want lightning to strike me

Right in my forgiving mind.

I want the whole world to hear

How I, with utter trepidation

Got over my fears

Was brave AF

And let you throw me away again.

Jennie Allida Dickenson

This foolishness has to be seen.

A fable for the ages

May all the other stupid girls learn.

If he wanted to.

He would.

Jennie Allida Dickenson

Heart Break

I am trying to be really tough.

And not let my heart break.

Every time I suffer some heartache

From a failed romance

My left arm hurts

Tingles

My left hand is numb as I type this

I have tried everything to get feeling back to it

It's been hours now.

I should go to the ER

They would tell me

I am having a psychotic break

Give me some drugs

Send me to an institution because I was crying over a modern man.

This is me trying not to be broken-hearted!

The last time I felt broken hearted

Legit I was grasping at my chest

Extreme pain.

I am probably having mini heart attacks

The poor thing is tired

Strained

Yet still finds dumb hope

Jennie Allida Dickenson

An unfounded optimism.

But I really don't think it can take it

One more love

And utter disappointment

And the despair will send it convulsing

Ridiculous

So let it be known

No Money need be spent on autopsy

She died of unrequited love

Sexual trickery

Flagrant disregard

And please don't mark the grave

I'd rather not be visited

by any repentants.

Or pissers.

Don't even hold a fucking wake.

Jennie Allida Dickenson

Look At Me

I am so stupid.

If you wanted I would drive there in a heartbeat.

I would blaze all my gas up to spend an hour or two

A hotel room in some random East Texas town.

Despite the fact you won't text me back

When the tone has even a hint of confrontation in it.

You have already trained me

DONT ask for any sort confirmation that you return my adoration.

I already know I should exist on the barest minimum of affection.

The sick and sad part is

Your bare minimum of affection is a flood for me.

The famine I have survived makes

A couple texts a day seem like a feast of attention.

I am obviously getting out of line

By asking for more

Ungrateful wretch wants to see you in person.

Disgusting.

I should be stronger

All this makes me feel like a beggar

Even though I will spend all my money to get it.

An addict.

Jennie Allida Dickenson

For the tiniest respect.

There are times of the month you treat me like I am dirty and wrong.

Like my gift of creation is disgusting.

You won't touch me.

And when I ask more

I am crazy.

Stupid.

Because I can tell you don't love me.

So why the fuck

Do you kiss me?

How can you look at me?

Jennie Allida Dickenson

YEET

Shot myself again

Always in the most terrible most painful ways

Never fatally

Self sabotage

Feeling undeserving

Worthless

I could list all the ways I brought it on myself

This heartache

But the reality is I YEET

Myself off the cliff

Before anyone can ever choose me

I fear loneliness

So I give it to myself

I reject myself before anyone else can

I want a man

Spiritual and kind

Who can help elevate my life

Whose mere presence would be a support

And then I jump off fucking cliffs

And not a one has ever asked me to stay.

Jennie Allida Dickenson

Mars on the Warpath

I don't know why I am flipping out.

He is literally the best man I know.

Handsome strong

Level headed

Calm

And I am acting out

I went from chill

To %5000

I think he is cheating on me

Because I know he has an IG

Because there was a Loretta Lynn

Song on the radio and he said her voice was sexy.

And when someone won't drive 15 minutes out of their way to see you.

You start to wonder 🗯

Have all my efforts been for naught!?!?

But he texts me everyday

Kept me alive for a couple days

I am so in love

That the terror of abandonment

Is far greater than it has ever been

I have already been devising plans to keep him alive for the next hundred years!

Jennie Allida Dickenson

Appealing to all the gods on his behalf

And graciously thanking them for every moment!

I suppose that's why I feel this way

If I didn't need any reassurance

Maybe this would work?

Is that one sided?

Lopsided like I feel the desire is

I have far more initiative.

But I also can sympathize

He is a young man. 33

And I am an old woman. 33

He could have the world

If he wasn't distracted by me

Could work hard

Have a family at a riper

Older more successful age.

And I have already been exposed to the elements.

Sun burnt, freckled.

Scarred, pocked,

Diseased, broken.

Wisened,

Healed a dozen to a hundred and witchy thousand handfuls of time.

There could be something

More new

Jennie Allida Dickenson

A soul he hasn't met in life quite yet.

Tiring of the same old story

Mars on the warpath

Maybe true love

Is being forgiven

By your worst enemy

And becoming family.

Nature is polarity.

Shared experience

Reveals duality.

Jennie Allida Dickenson

97.1 Country Gold

Low on the horizon,

The moon was a thin bowl

Orange in the winter night.

A waxing crescent that you had called

God's thumbprint.

Your concern and care for me

As fresh on my mind as

The taste of your lips on mine.

My legs still a bit shaky

As I pressed the clutch to shift into fifth.

Cruising 190 westward home.

The beautiful clear starry night

Seen from the canyon that the road carved between the pines.

I contemplated the moon,

The evening,

Your eyes looking into mine.

As 97.1 country gold played romantic song

After romantic song

Lyrics echoing the tenderness I was savoring.

Wind whistling in the cracked window

Bracing breeze to keep me present.

Jennie Allida Dickenson

The ease and excitement of our new beginning.

The joy even at our parting temporarily.

I drove remembering;

Cataloging the feeling:

Your looks, words, touch, kindness and acceptance.

And the moon watched me

Dream all sorts of hypothetical

Beautiful things.

Excited at the prospect of going East on 190.

Jennie Allida Dickenson

Late February

I am driving down 1375 over lake Conroe with the windows down

it's 77 degrees

The Texas piney woods smells like East Texas should

We are both in locales far from home

yet near in this expansive state

Work trips

Organizing dirt and cataloging birds

Stewards of the land that separates us

Working hard

Sweating

 trying to save a dime off each dollar

For a plot of it to call our own

I will have a whole purple fence

Serious

Sacred

As the time apart I am making intentional

To become myself at her best

I respect your rest

Integrating

The possibility of life's best

Intentionally building my will

Stressing my body stronger

Leaning into responsibility

Realizing I have love to live for

Not to just expend

Jennie Allida Dickenson

But to spend

At least a dime off a dollar on myself

That wonderfully includes

A masculine half

Polarity a dance and a snap

I am learning:

You taught me to use first gear

Manually transmitted

And a trick!

 gently coaxing back up

Taming my reverse slapstick

Saving my clutch

From grinding gears

How to relax

Be whole

Sit on the couch and watch a movie

Sleep early and soundly

Step back

The flame starts with nurture

Not my oil soaked rags as fuel

Tender kindling

Gentle breath

And the burn of realizations

Fire like tan tien

Is spirit never ending

Even though it's embodying

Jennie Allida Dickenson

Shivers through you

Searing flesh tightens

Revealing vulnerable selves through the cracks

You felt calm and strong.

A bloom of trust

Awakened in me,

My chest felt like a cavern

Where it had opened up.

A secret undiscovered.

The feeling of security so alien to me.

Finding a treasure I had long desired.

With the finding

It became truly prized.

Oh how I wanted to cry!

And tell you I love you.

Instead I wrapped you tightly

In an embrace

Showered you with kisses

And told you,

I trust you

I trust you

I trust you.

Jennie Allida Dickenson

Google Search Rant

I could scroll all the memes and advice,

all the yoga moves and manifesting tricks

and never make a difference.

I came here to enjoy an evening and relax and y'all making me feel bad.

Gone is the television that's free.

Ads have gotten to everything.

There is no mindless accompaniment

It's all advertising and subtle brainwashing

Till your thighs are chafed from rubbing

Your spine is out of alignment

Even your relaxing is not quite

And the lighting to see by not cutting edge

Can't we just take an evening off with friends?

Can I look at baby pictures?

Promotions and troubles

And gratitude

Without your need to sell me booty enhancing leggings that will apparently save the relationship

you can also sell me with the expando package on how to fix it?

Plus the psychic to tell me how it's going

and the plant medicine retreat

and life coach to integrate what the fuck just happened to me?

Jennie Allida Dickenson

Maybe a vacation in Tulum will fix you?

I tell you that I want to go to Siberia on vacation.

Riddle me why they don't try to sell me that?

Why don't they know I actually want a job as a dishwasher in Malta?

Has google ever considered my real feelings?

They show me things some sad desperate 33 year old single white woman should want.

What if I want those things and a surprise.

Take the punch out of life by making it too available. I want to search.

Suggest doing heroin in Belarus for once google.

Y'all are always selling me ayahuasca in Peru.

What about deadly nightshade and mushrooms 🍄?

What about simply death.

Why does it boil down to the sex you can't get me.

The attraction you can't get me, the love you can't get me.

Nothing actually comes from you.

Can you please let your algorithm stop being so helpful.

I think it's limiting the hand of fate. So please

(and not kindly, thank you much)

Fuck off.

Jennie Allida Dickenson

PATRIARCH

Halfway between the vultures and the pecan tree I built the pyre.

The stars were brighter than anywhere in Texas I'd ever seen.

I fed the flames the half wrought projects of my grandfather's creativity.

Crying at the thought of a life unfinished

Yet consciously jealous of one so full.

Well lived, well traveled

And full of love and light

Service and self sacrifice

So well wrought.

And as souls do:

Preciously bought.

Such is life.

In general.

daughter

granddaughter

It's pressure and responsibility

The empathy made me

Brutal and caring

Hardened and soft

War torn beauty and peaceful chaos

I keep it exciting

Jennie Allida Dickenson

I thrive on my gift

And I am the gift itself

My patriarchy is the only reason I am still alive

I couldn't bear them knowing I gave them up and quit.

So I am stalwart.

They are the tree

I am the fruit.

The fruit becoming the tree.

Stories live inside of me

Ready to unfold with the ear

when I birth it.

I hope my creation is as creative

Live such a complete wonderful life.

Have as many pursuits.

Enjoyments and pastimes

Children and life.

Jennie Allida Dickenson

The Answer is Violence

I have a man that demands perfect answers out of me after I have been awake

For 20 hours and worked 13 of them.

Minor foibles in tone or messaging get brutal over standing measures of disassociation and disregard.

I may do this day after day back to back

he won't respect the "it's not too cold to suffer clause."

And it costs me a dime.

He says he wants to wake up in a good mood.

I wake up to the fresh hell

Of everything I have to accomplish in such a short time.

I get accused of stomping around too purposely.

Exacting my demands of the day too violently.

Preoccupied with mass genocide to care about how he feels about me sonically.

When I need someone to sympathize with.

Another warrior to talk to.

He tries to dominate me like the dog he is training.

He eventually can't take the weather

I would concede.

He never fights for me, blames and shames.

And it will never cause my submission.

I thought he'd realize at some point.

The answer is violence.

Jennie Allida Dickenson

Which/Witch

I called myself "witch".

I wanted power

Knowledge

I learnt nothing is ever easy.

Intercession,

Favor!

Costs the Gods just as much as our "Intercession" does

when we do it for each other ~

Favored or favorite.

Your Grandma was emulating GOD

My grandmothers have taught me,

My mothers have modeled it for me.

Is there a choice of which?

Jennie Allida Dickenson

Berries

A bushel of overly ripe strawberries.
Just one in the corner molding.
Compared to you I am under ripe.
No matter how fresh I get with you.
If I got hit with enough sunshine
I might turn sweet enough for your tooth.
The hankering however is on my part.
I am at the apex of my color and flavor.
I wish you would pick me clean.

Jennie Allida Dickenson

Thrill of the Grill

A flitting shadow of your wheel beyond the sharp corner of the end of the block.
Looking up to see you from where I was hiding behind the coca cola cooler.
You looked around halfway up to the counter
And about faced quickly.
I looked at our pizza, the crowd and understood and followed you out
I didn't want to call out as I had seen you earlier
And wanted to think you hadn't seen me at all.
Makes me feel like I was prowling
But who is the prey?
How many times a week are you going to come get a slice of pizza?
I can think all crazy like I know you.
And we are meant to be,
Make designs about you because you haven't let me down yet.
I don't want to find out.
What would you do if I suddenly popped around a corner
And confronted you?

Jennie Allida Dickenson

Fillmore and Broadway

Standing at the top of Fillmore and Broadway
I light up. 10:50. The sun is perfect
Shining on the ruffled bay under the Golden Gate.
I realize; sun and wind dried curls whipping my brain.
I should be viewing this vista differently.
Valuing my work for myself
Stepping down the sidewalk long awkward gaits,
2 steps at a time past million dollar condos
To go to work as a cashier for a pizza joint that doesn't respect my frankness.
I should be walking up those stairs.
Imperious into the fog and wind
Sun gleaming off of me.
I knew
ESP style
My wish granted that day.
And I hiked back up.

Jennie Allida Dickenson

Unfolding Mystery

She told me I would recognize his spirit.
He told me to feel his hands
As he gently grabbed my belt.
She told me he has been watching me.
And this evening I had him coming back for more.
She told me he would have dark curly hair.
He told me exactly what he wanted.
Waltzed in wearing high water overalls
And charmed a kiss from me.
She told me I would have to keep him intellectually stimulated.
I told him to call me
Written hastily on a pizza box.
A disconnected Nevada number.
He pulled away in a scooby doo green van.
Leaving me wondering who are you?
Rather than where.
A mystery unfolding.

Jennie Allida Dickenson

This Book

It was where you could fit a pen into a book comfortably.
Closing shut to encompass the thoughts to be manifested later.
Here is where my mind starts functioning properly again
With enough booze and weed.
Where I feel a rising pang of the more whole version of my mind
Calling to the harried fraction of me.
On a motorized use wash repeat cycle.
A smoke brush eat repeat.
A work play sleep.
This book needs to be a daily template
A place to record and therefore learn my lessons.
A journal of the hard knocks
So I don't repeat
A step forward, ever forward
To being more conscious.

Jennie Allida Dickenson

Fall Season

In the season when all the wasps get delirious and lackadaisical.
You left me before snow could sprinkle passes.
Staying long enough for nights to chill
and sandals to be impractical.
A bloom in my heart
When leaves turnt as golden as your embraces.
Holding on as tightly as the pears to the tree
Before they start falling.
Like I have been
With you in love.
And you mentioned
How you didn't want it to stop
The free fall.
I think it is a continuous process,
With the first real bite of cold air
With the drifting leaves of fall.

Jennie Allida Dickenson

Rocket

She told me she felt like a rocket ready to go off.
The image of her shaking with the gathering power of lift off
Didn't make me laugh.
10…9…..8…
I felt this room we shared was a den
The door a shadowed opening
From which the evil radiated down the hall
Dispersed into the sky
7…6…5…
I blew out our candle
The smoke floats to her
Drawn in through her nostrils
It clouds her
Thick could be cut with a knife
Sending gray tendrils spiraling
4…3..
Will I wake with purpose?
Slide into shoes out the door while she sleeps
Her smokey eyes blinking to noon light
2…1..
She sees I am gone.

Jennie Allida Dickenson

Song Three

With straight up intention
I was able to find you
In the sea of fifty thousand
We sweat it out to be purified
And sleep together
Bathed in waxing gibbous light.
But I haven't caught you
Here on the high desert
You kick scream and fight
Silently you deman the love I send
Inside my hard work
You absolutley refuse to bend.
I can't think of more I could do
No helping hand to lend.
Pre occupied with adventure
You refuse to embark
On the most dangerous of all.
Loving me to the end.

Jennie Allida Dickenson

Thank You

Thank you God for my misery.
Thank you for sending
the most perfect exemplary being of my desires
Then not letting me have him.
Thank you for forcing me to grow
For forcing me to improve
In order to win him over.
Thank you for the misery
Of the absolute knowing I have.
Thank you for terror that I wont be succesful.
Thank you for the misery
Of being rejected over and over again.
Thank you for the complete dejection
I feel when he puts me off again.
Thank you for the misery of my imagination
That creates delusions of a wonderous life
If he would just accept me.
Thank you for knowing better than I do.

Jennie Allida Dickenson

Fireworks

There were no fireworks tonight.
Today doused cooly
Something I didn't take well
My usually sharp mind
Failing to come back conversely
At all from the shock
Of his tactfully curt diffusement
Of my very short
Very flammable fuse.
An internal display of hurt colored
Gunpowder burst
Inside spontaneous
Human combustion
My shrapnel punctured heart
Bleeding an energetic acetylene gas
That when I drink this gas station gin
Smoke a pity cig
Will ignite
The blast sending me off in any direction
Aiming my tires, horn and antique bike
Down fifth street
See how far this unseen
Fire display sends me.

Jennie Allida Dickenson

Doll

You are such a doll.
Sometimes I have an intense
Urge to grab you
Love you and coo.
I have a feeling
You'd like the attention
But brush me off
Briskly perhaps
Gruffly. It's a chance.
And I am not that brave around you.
Not a matter of guts
But that is where it would hurt.
My gut reaction
To the put off
A real sickness to the put down
So I torture myself
With just thinking
Of your course of action
If I jumped you right now
Coddled
And tickled your old bones.

Jennie Allida Dickenson

Bow and Arrow Fuck You Style

For awhile there I didn't have
Enough self respect to try
To ask you to stop treating
Me like a dog.
But I have been angry enough
To tear everuthing apart
Tie it back up again
Like a red ribbon in my braid
Stomp it down
Shoot it into a cloud
Bow and arrow fuck you style
Till there is nothing
Left to be said!

Jennie Allida Dickenson

Little Sisters

I'd like to make an accounting
Of the many bruises and scratches
I have suffered for you
How I lost a precious ring
And tore my favorite pants
The ring slipping off my furiously paddling hands
As I tried to catch up to save you.
And a short but heartbreaking rip
As I scrambled up nearly vertical rock to reach you.
Each time
Maybe because of my vigilance
You were safe
But each time it felt a false alarm.
And how could you say I don't love you?!
After all I didn't beat on you
Or ask you not to alarm me again.
Because I do care
Skin purple and blue
And I will do it again soon
You and all the others are weights
Rocks in my pockets.
But you and the others
Are how I got this strong.

Jennie Allida Dickenson

Set Free On The Wind

On a tide pool investigation
Hopping at low tide
To see hermit crabs and starfish
We found a family out spreading ashes
They let their ashes fly
Before I had assessed their intentions
I was gracefully trying to exit the vicinity
When the high winds shifted my way
I carried part of the bereaved away
In my new black wool jacket
A gray stain of the cloud that brought him here
He jumped out of the bag
Like a wild hare on his way back to town
Free from his family
Free of his mortal remains
And truly able to travel
from his primordial spiritual tide pool.

Jennie Allida Dickenson

The Green of my Gold

No more basement gloom
Celebration
Exaltation
Of space and work
The damp musty smells of production
Like green money in leather wallets
Not green jealousy
And my affections returned a salt lick
A cuttlefish to sharpen my beak
Sharp enough to cut me
Criticism matters
And I am taking it to heart
Especially my own
So where it started
Will be the place where roots grow
To cover the wounds gouged deep
Like stitches
A way for me to get out
Get out of here soon
On the green of my gold.

Jennie Allida Dickenson

DONT WALK

I stopped a moment
My babble over my americano
To study your face
Eyes reddened and rubbed
I look down not wanting
You to notice that I know.
Let's walk.
Arm around my shoulder
Neon lights around the block
The sun so warm
Christmas music playing on the 30th
Downtown Reno
I said goodbye today
Tight lipped
Seeping corners of your eyes
I try to be delightful to lighten the mood
To stop welling tears
But make them more stark
Against my bared grinning teeth
Waiting for the cross walk signal
Timing our departure from company.
WALK

Jennie Allida Dickenson

2nd Day of Spring

Bugs are my ever present friends
Now crawling into my bed more readily than I
Fresh scrubbed pots drying slowly
Languid unsqueezed sponges
Microbial full bloom
The air is sweet with a million tiny flowers
Trees planted in hope
A plan only in dreams
Where strange guests
Parade over property lines
Long desert vistas
Under purple skies
Where old lovers reunite
The long season at its tipping point
Wind brushing away dusty doubt
Silver green pollen
Settling onto everything
Filling the fractures of the day
Sitting on the porch
Staring into space
Till the ant bites
The dead branches falling
Startling cracks at dusk
Dogs barking late into the night.

Jennie Allida Dickenson

Terrorist

All I am getting out of my quest
Is a lot of empty hard packs
And cigarette butts.
Frustration and desperation
Are pins on my left and right breast
An alert to passerbys.
I left snide slightly dramatic
Messages on your new phone.
Furthering from my first trenches
Far from mysterious
Hiding in caves in high mountains
Cowering in the Caucasus.
Showering you with terrorist
Like acts of my affections.

Jennie Allida Dickenson

Jungle Man

Classically a heartbreaker. That face.
And you a modern day renaissance man
I could understand how you stole
Making off with things
I couldn't believe you got your hands on.
Asking me out to dinner then feeding me lifted food from your bag.
I could understand your need
Our situation echoing each other
I was fed off your criminal
And I felt under your vigilante protection.
You stole my imagination
Because I loved the idea of you.
Hoping you would save me
From the delicately explosive situation
I had worked my way into.
I hoped your tarzan like view of good and right
Would swoop me up from the pit of forked tongues
I was so cautiously treading about.
But as I wasn't Jane
My secret ways of communicating
This never got past more than hopeless signaling.
Though I realized
When you'd completely ignore me
For a rainbow
A good picture to be taken
To climb a tree
Or to be pepper sprayed at a protest
That you didn't need the distraction in me.

Jennie Allida Dickenson

Jam on it Honey

Now how did you think it would pan out?
Did you expect…
What? Broken glass
Laughing and understanding
Or drunkenness induced
By our discomfort
Sidelong glances
Wondering at what I was after
What I was going to do
Wandering motives
And am I the axle?
Here with orbiting single serving
Jams and one honey package
The ones I'll open
And spread on this stiff toast
Never being satiated
By the burnt crust
Of who is really getting burned here.
A fire spreading to the middle
In from spokes
Who is starting it?
And why do you want to be
My orange marmalade?
To see how mired I am in the honey.
Slowing me down.

Jennie Allida Dickenson

Handbag

Sitting pretty in the crook of her arm
Your position as handbag
Is straining you unclasped.
You want to slip into the
thief hands of unsurety.
Away from her showing you off.
Stowing her precious essentials
And most used objects in you.
Where as I want a position as such
Seeking someone to be sure of.
To know someone will fill
And consume the contents of this decanter.
Instead of shooting straight
From the bottle and leaving it half empty.
This struggle at different extremes
Could resolve itself
So I propose..
After we tally all the points
We earned
Not counting
To see who is on top
And who lost in our sick game
We can meet in the middle
On friendly terms
Belt line
We'll cinch eachother up
You be the hands on hips
I've been missing
And I won't store anything in you.

Jennie Allida Dickenson

He

Intimidated me
And I liked it.
A pawn with whom I exacted revenge.
Pawned with my first taste,
I found craving.
I wanted to be healed
But played the game so wrong
Exposing my queen
And knowing now as
Checkmate approaches
My advances will just be
Hopelessly countered.

Jennie Allida Dickenson

Texas to Tennessee

He thinks of me nearly everyday he says.
Everyday a thought cosmically spillt in my direction.
He doesn't know where I am
Or where my home is
And I didn't forget to say goodbye.
I left in a hurry
Tired of my failed attempts
To make friends realize
I was fleeting.
Don't expect me
But don't lock your doors.
Could I make it your way?
Toward the Mississippi I've never seen?
Now having lost my knack for
Huckleberry adventure to a Finn
If I was what I boasted
I would be out there with a 45
Borrowed hand cannon
Hitching my way on 80 East
To Tennessee
Instead of taken care of
Gaining weight to others worry.
I sit poolside guilting my grandfather
Over cigs and the beers we're sharing.
Hiding my shame from my straight laced sisters.
My love of funk
Rotating out for a more
Twangy banjo music
That echoes the bug calls

Jennie Allida Dickenson

I fall asleep to at night.
My well fed exhausted body
Peeling layers of paranoia
Like sunburned skin.
Troubling dreams of home
That scrub my inside different.
And the friends I have made
In the last nine months
Never enter my dreams
And hardly ever dance
Through my cognizant reality
But in my absurd stories.

Jennie Allida Dickenson

Epiphany

It had faded from purple to white.
When it still held the color
Of your lavender smell
White moths crossed my path
Hexing the steps I was taking
Tying the packaging ribbon to my wrist
She told me that
I'd have an epiphany
After it had fallen off naturally
Very seriously and ceremoniously
Touching my left wrist
In the sunny yellow kitchen.
I thought it would fall off soon
Or soon enough
For me to catch time with you.
A year later
After washing through my troubles
And fun with me
It fell off.
The sun warming us as it fell
Sitting out front smoking cigs
And feeling hints of what I needed,
Wanted, before.
Forgotten in times away
Explaining why I wasn't able
To hear anything about that time.
Hey, you remember it?

Jennie Allida Dickenson

Back when I was rash enough
Bold enough to steal
Or comfortable enough.
Our conversation never
Really touching on what
I wanted to say.
My epiphany left a sterile
White searing tan line
Where my courage used to be.
An epiphany of how
I wanted you
And you.
Never me.

Jennie Allida Dickenson

My Cool

10/6/2008

I've got to keep the cool,
I shroud myself in
When I walk,
A stride,
Purposefully
A strut.
To inject my self confidence
With a brisk step.
To keep a positive mental attitude.
A bounce with my own beat.
Singing and only sort of caring
Who overhears.
Belting when I am alone.
Trying to undo the mental stress.
Worrying about many regrets.
Wearing cool like a hood,
Blinders and sun catchers
Ignoring the bad and the good.

Jennie Allida Dickenson

Ambiguity

Ambiguity
Has me looking up,
Under my own shoes.
In boxes I already know the contents of
Searching for what?
I can't remember now.
Hoping to recognize it when I find it.
Ambiguity hiding as golden whiskey
Till the glass is empty.
Your words drip ambiguity.
They came out of the say nothing bible.
The give her no hope version.
Ambiguity has settled
Where it feels like my veins.
A maze of blood highways
Taking me nowhere.
Asking me all those questions I hate to answer.
With, "I don't know"
Loose plans
Unsent letters.
Finding and realizing
He will never be yours again.

Jennie Allida Dickenson

Anxiety

Anxiety
Floats over me
A net dropped on my head
If it was tangible
I would gnaw my way out.
Anxiety the color of
Another darkening sky
Makes me grind my teeth
Clench my jaw
The anxiety
of knowing exactly what you have to do.
A mental list so long
If I write it down
I will overwhelm myself.

Jennie Allida Dickenson

I-80

Nevada is inexplicably beautiful.
The 18-wheeler kicked up a cloud of dust
That we could see trailing five miles away
As we zoomed 80 miles per hour toward it.
The kitty litter plant smelling faintly of onions.
The only building to be seen for fifteen miles.
The tawny ridges like a long ago frozen wave
A ripple in the geological time of this ancient place.
Far off on the horizon a range of mountains seem to be blue mist
And the wind whipped clouds scutter by far above.
I want to write our names with the rocks on the side of I-80.
Where the salty soil has cracked and split.
A reflection of us.
A constellation of broken glass
Of some tragic collision.
What could have been.

Jennie Allida Dickenson

Jennie Allida Dickenson

Made in the USA
Columbia, SC
27 November 2024